I WILL NOT GO
TO MARKET TODAY

by HARRY ALLARD
Pictures by JAMES MARSHALL

THE DIAL PRESS · NEW YORK

Published by
The Dial Press
1 Dag Hammarskjold Plaza
New York, New York 10017

First printing
Design by Atha Tehon

Library of Congress Cataloging in Publication Data
Allard, Harry
I will not go to market today.
Summary: Fenimore B. Buttercrunch's repeated
attempts to go to market are met with obstacles.
[1. Shopping—Fiction] I. Marshall, James, 1942—
II. Title.
PZ7.A413Iac   [E]   78-72474
ISBN 0-8037-4019-0
ISBN 0-8037-4020-4 lib. bdg.

For Ken Raymond
and Victoria Frese

Fenimore B. Buttercrunch awoke one morning to
find there was no jam for his morning toast and tea.
"No jam!" he said. "I must go to market today."

Fenimore B. Buttercrunch looked out
the window. There was a blizzard raging.
"I cannot go to market today," he said.

Dreaming of jam, he warmed
his tootsies by the fire.

The next day there was a heat wave.

"Too hot to go to market today," Fenimore said.

"Off to market today!"
said Fenimore the next day.

But heavy fog forced him home.

"There's no reason not to go to market today,"
thought Fenimore B. Buttercrunch,
stepping out of his bubble bath the next day.

But a hurricane nearly blew
Buttercrunch away.

The next day Fenimore B. Buttercrunch was
in his kitchen thinking that nothing could
stop him from going to market that day.

Suddenly the house began to shake.
"An earthquake!" screamed Fenimore.
He did not go to market that day.

At nine thirty the next morning,
just as Fenimore B. Buttercrunch was
locking his front door...

...the dam broke.
"If it isn't one thing, it's another,"
thought Fenimore.

"Perfect weather today," said the weatherman.
"Off to market!" said Fenimore.

However, there was a mean dinosaur
sitting in the front yard.
"Hmmm..." said Fenimore, closing the door.

"There's no reason not to go to
market today," said Fenimore as he
brushed his teeth the next day.

But Fenimore had not gone two blocks before
he found himself caught in a traffic jam.
"This isn't the jam I had in mind," he said.

That night Fenimore B. Buttercrunch
went to bed early.
"I must get a good night's rest if I am to go
to market tomorrow," he said.

He peeked out the door the next morning.

The coast was clear.

"It's off to market today!" he sang.

As he was going down the front steps,
Fenimore caught his foot in his shopping bag,
fell, and broke his right leg.

He was laid up for six months.
"I just don't seem to have any luck,"
he said to himself.

At last Fenimore B. Buttercrunch was
well enough to get up and walk.
"Hi-ho, it's off to market today!" he sang
one morning, stepping over a stile.

But, oh! Whom should he run into but his
gabby Aunt Ethel-Mae Buttercrunch-Jones.
"I'm late for a dental appointment,"
he fibbed, and hurried off down the road.

Fenimore B. Buttercrunch made it to market
just before closing time.

"I'd like a jar of jam," he said.

"Raspberry?" asked the clerk.

"No, strawberry," said Fenimore.

"I do so like jam with my toast and my tea,"
said Fenimore B. Buttercrunch.